Rockets

STAN THE DOG

Stan and the
Sneaky Snacks

Scoular Anderson

A & C Black • London

For Ailsa

Rockets series:
CROOK CATCHERS - Karen Wallace & Judy Brown
HAUNTED MOUSE - Dee Shulman
LITTLE T - Frank Rodgers
MOTLEY'S CREW - Margaret Ryan &
Margaret Chamberlain
MR CROC - Frank Rodgers
MRS MAGIC - Wendy Smith
MY FUNNY FAMILY - Colin West
ROVER - Chris Powling & Scoular Anderson
SILLY SAUSAGE - Michaela Morgan & Dee Shulman
SPACE TWINS - Wendy Smith
STAN THE DOG - Scoular Anderson
WIZARD'S BOY - Scoular Anderson

First paperback edition 2003
First published 2002 by A & C Black Publishers Ltd
37 Soho Square, London W1D 3QZ
www.acblack.com

Text and illustrations copyright © 2002 Scoular Anderson

The right of Scoular Anderson to be identified as author
and illustrator of this work has been asserted by him
in accordance with the Copyright, Designs and Patents Act 1988.

ISBN 0-7136-6143-7

A CIP catalogue record for this book is available
from the British Library.

A & C Black uses paper produced with elemental
chlorine-free pulp, harvested from managed sustainable forests.

Printed and bound by G. Z. Printek, Bilbao, Spain.

First Helping

It was the weekend so Stan was happy.
All the family were at home. Stan had his
own names for his family. Bigbelly and
Canopener didn't go to work on weekends.
Crumble and Handout didn't go to school
either so there would be more food around.

Stan waited for everyone to get up.

Bigbelly was the first one to come downstairs.

He opened the back door to let Stan out.

Stan wandered down the garden, sniffing.

SNIFF
SNIFF

He did what
he was supposed
to do.

He went on to the back gate and peered into the lane.

The school kids took a short cut through the lane so there were always bits of food lying around.

Bigbelly had put a high latch on the gate to stop Stan getting out into the lane.

Stan checked that no one was looking.

He reached up...

...flicked the latch...

CLICK!

...and went out into the lane.

Stan ate the half-hamburger.

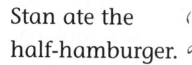

He found a crisp packet with several crisps still in it.

He found a green pastille.

Then he found a blob of dried ice cream which he licked.

After his snack he wandered back into the garden and pushed the gate shut.

He stopped at the bird table.

He pushed open the back door and walked into the kitchen.

Second Helping

Bigbelly had cooked himself some bacon for breakfast. Crumble and Handout were already at the table eating cereal and toast. Stan took up his usual place under the table.

Crumble was dropping crumbs everywhere. There were already quite a few for Stan to lick up.

He knew he'd get a handout from Handout so he sat very close.

Suddenly there was a horrible shriek.

Canopener had arrived.

In a flash, Stan was out from under the
table and standing beside his bowl.

But the bacon went into the bin.

Stan went back under the table.

The family carried on with breakfast.

After breakfast, Stan went to doze in his bed. He was having a lovely dream when...

...he was woken up by a noise.

"RATTLE! CHINK!

That sounds like my lead! But we NEVER go for a walk on Saturday mornings!

But Stan was wrong.

Eh?

STAN! WALKIES!

Bigbelly was standing in the hall holding his lead.

Stan was horrified.

Bigbelly took Stan out of the back door.
The rest of the family came to see them
off.

Bigbelly jogged
down the garden,
out of the
back gate and
into the lane.

Third Helping

Jogging with Bigbelly wasn't much fun.
His big feet went flip, flap, flip, flap on
the ground.

FLIP!

FLAP!

His belly went
wobble, wobble,
wobble.

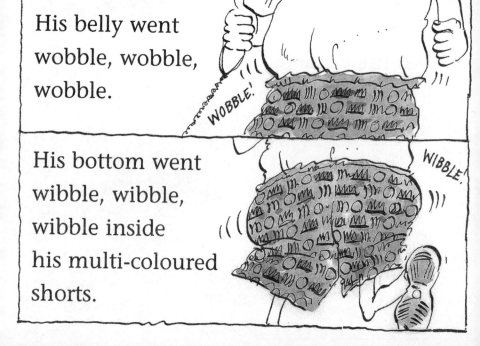

WOBBLE!

His bottom went
wibble, wibble,
wibble inside
his multi-coloured
shorts.

WIBBLE!

By the time they got to the end of the
lane, Bigbelly was already out of breath
and red in the face.

Bigbelly rummaged in one of the pockets of his shorts and brought out some...

He rummaged in the other pocket.

Just then, Bigbelly dropped something
and Stan leapt forward.

But he was in for a big disappointment.

Bigbelly was not pleased.

Bigbelly got on the move again. It was more of a walk than a jog. They went down the street and turned left at the traffic lights.

Hang on! This isn't the way to the park.

It was the way to Dino's café.

Bigbelly tied Stan's lead to a table.

He went into the café.

Bigbelly was taking ages and Stan was getting bored. A woman passed, eating a packet of crisps.

She threw the packet into a litter bin.

It teetered on the edge.

Then it fell out.

Stan stretched to reach the crisps...

...but a gust of wind blew the packet away.

Stan really wanted that packet.

Inside the café, Bigbelly was just finishing his bacon and eggs. He saw something out of the corner of his eye through the window.

The umbrella moved one way then back the other way.

Then it toppled over and caught one of the hanging baskets as it fell.

There was a thump then a bang then a shriek. Bigbelly leapt up from his table.

Bigbelly got Stan out from the mess,
then they walked quickly home
through the park.

The family were waiting for their return.

Fourth Helping

Stan was lying in his basket having another lovely dream.

And if you answer this question right you win a million cans of DOGZO!

It was Sunday morning. The family wouldn't be up for ages and ages.

Then Stan heard two noises he didn't
like. The first noise came from the
bathroom.
Someone
was up.

GURGLE...
..GURRRGLE...
...FLUSSSH!

He thought he had better check out the
second noise. He walked down the hall
and into the sitting room. He climbed up
onto a chair by the window.

Rain!
I thought so.
I'm not going
out in that!

On the way back to the kitchen Stan got a shock. There was Bigbelly.

They went out of the back door and headed for the park this time.

Stan was miserable. Bigbelly's feet splashed in all the puddles.

Jogging wasn't fun. There was no time to stop and sniff at interesting things.

They had just come round the corner
of the shed by the pond when Stan
spotted something.

Stan stopped.

The lead slipped out of Bigbelly's hand and he flew forward.

He skidded in a puddle and took a dive over the park bench.

Bigbelly was not pleased.

Stan turned and ran.

He dodged past Pongo and Fangs.

He didn't stop running until he was safely back home.

37

Fifth Helping

When Bigbelly got home he was exhausted. He had chased Stan all the way. Canopener sorted out his bumps and bruises.

Canopener wasn't going to let Bigbelly off the hook.

After lunch came Stan's favourite moment of the day. Canopener took out a can opener and opened a can of Dogzo.

After that, the family was busy. Bigbelly washed the car.

Canopener tidied the garden.

Crumble and Handout played football.

Normally, Stan liked to play football too but he was worried about another jog. He wasn't comfy in his bed.

He wasn't comfy on the sofa.

He wandered from room to room,

He was walking down the hall when he saw a red light blinking on the telephone.

Stan pressed a button...

...then listened to the message.

Stan found
this message
very interesting.

Later in the afternoon, Canopener got
in the car and went out.

Bigbelly was
reading the
Sunday papers.

Crumble and
Handout were playing
a computer game.

Stan knew it was his walkies time. He stood beside Bigbelly and whined.

Eventually, Stan had to take drastic action.

Bigbelly wasn't in a good mood. The children had been dragged away from their game so they weren't in a good mood either.

Stan kept dragging them the opposite way from the park.

Stan pulled them all the way to Dino's.

They pressed their noses against the window.

There was a bit of an argument when they got back into the car.

Once they were back home, the family set off again, jogging to the park. Stan was happy to let them go.